WALT DISNEY PRODUCTIONS
presents

Merry Christmas, Uncle Scrooge McDuck!

Random House New York

Book Club Edition

 Published in the United States by Random House, Inc., New York, and simultaneously in Canada by Random House of Canada Limited, Toronto. Originally published in Denmark as ONKEL JOAKIM REDDER JULEN by Gutenberghus Bladene, Copenhagen. ISBN: 0-394-84781-4 (trade); 0-394-94781-9 (lib. bdg.) Manufactured in the United States of America
4 5 6 7 8 9 0 B C D E F G H I J K

Christmas was coming.

Everyone was busy shopping.

Everyone but Donald Duck.

Donald was busy working.

Donald's boss, Uncle Scrooge McDuck, made him work long and hard.

Uncle Scrooge hated Christmas.

He looked at the Christmas shoppers from his big sleigh.

"Christmas! Bah! Humbug!" he said.

Uncle Scrooge lived in the biggest house in town.

He never walked home from work.

But poor Donald always walked.

He had no money for a sleigh.

He had no money for Christmas presents.

He did not even have money for a real Christmas tree.

Grandma Duck and Daisy Duck knew Donald was poor.

"We do not need money to have a merry Christmas," said Grandma Duck.

She was making their Christmas cake.

Huey, Dewey, and Louie could hardly wait to eat it.

Soon Uncle Donald would bring their tree.
"We will need lots of ornaments," said Dewey.

"And paper chains,"
said Daisy.

"And a Christmas-tree stand,"
said Huey and Louie.

Their cat was ready
for Christmas too.

Then Huey, Dewey, and Louie waited by the window.

They were waiting for their Uncle Donald. He would bring home a big Christmas tree.

At last Donald came back.

"Hi, Uncle Donald," said Dewey. "Where is our tree?"

"Right here," he said sadly.

They all looked at the tiny tree.

Daisy gave Donald some hot soup.

"The boys will be unhappy this Christmas. I have no money to buy presents for them," said Donald.

He was tired and cold.

"You must ask Uncle Scrooge for your pay ahead of time," said Daisy.

The next day Donald was at work very early.

"I need only a few dollars for presents," he said to himself. "And that mean old duck cannot scare me!"

Donald knocked softly on Uncle Scrooge's door.

"Please, Uncle Scrooge," began Donald, "can you give me some of my pay early? It is for Christmas presents."

The old duck glared at Donald.

"Money for Christmas? Bah! Humbug! Get back to work!" he snapped at Donald.

Donald worked all day.
He was tired and cold.
“Achoo!” sneezed Donald.

Then Donald walked home.
He saw beautiful trees.
And Christmas treats.

Uncle Scrooge went home too.
"Bah! Humbug!" he said.

Uncle Scrooge sat down to his lonely dinner.

"Christmas! Humbug!" he said.

Then he went upstairs to bed.
Soon he was fast asleep.

Uncle Scrooge had a dream.

In his dream, he saw himself as a boy.

It was Christmas.

What fun we used to have! he thought.

But that was a long, long time ago.

Uncle Scrooge woke up feeling happy.

Then he fell back to sleep.

He had another dream.
This time he was walking
in a strange part of town.

The houses were small and poor.
He stopped to look into a window.

Inside, Grandma Duck,
Daisy Duck, and the boys
were trimming a tiny tree.

Donald was sick in bed.

Uncle Scrooge heard them talking.

"It will be a sad Christmas for the boys. There are no presents and you are sick," said Grandma to Donald.

Then the boys went to Donald.
"Please get well, Uncle Donald,"
they said. "That is all we want
for Christmas."

A tear fell from Uncle Scrooge's eye.

Then Uncle Scrooge's dream ended.

He jumped out of his bed and ran to the window.

"Ho, there!" he called to the people below. "Is tonight Christmas Eve?"

"Yes," a man called back.

"Then it is not too late!" cried Uncle Scrooge.

He got dressed quickly and rushed off to the shops.

He bought the finest toys, the fastest trains, lots of candy. . .

the warmest caps
and robes, and the
prettiest Christmas
tree.

Uncle Scrooge knocked at Donald's door. "Merry Christmas!" said Uncle Scrooge.

Donald and the boys could hardly believe their eyes.

The boys gave Uncle Scrooge presents they had made.

Then Uncle Scrooge gave Donald one hundred dollars!

"You deserve it," he said. "You have been working hard."

Then they all trimmed the big tree.

The boys played with their new toys.

Uncle Scrooge raised his cup and said, “Merry Christmas to all of you.”

And it was the merriest Christmas ever.